The New Adventures of

MARY-KATE & ASHLEY™

The Case Of The

Weird Science Mystery

Look for more great books in

~The New Adventures of~
MARY-KATE & ASHLEY™

series:

and coming soon

The Case Of The
Weird Science Mystery

by Judy Katschke

📚HarperEntertainment
An Imprint of HarperCollins*Publishers*

A PARACHUTE PRESS BOOK

**PARACHUTE
PRESS**

Parachute Publishing, L.L.C.
156 Fifth Avenue
New York, NY 10010

DUALSTAR
PUBLICATIONS

Dualstar Publications
c/o Thorne and Company
A Professional Law Corporation
1801 Century Park East
Los Angeles, CA 90067

HarperEntertainment

An Imprint of HarperCollins*Publishers*
10 East 53rd Street, New York, NY 10022

10 9 8 7 6 5 4 3 2 1

THE SCIENCE FAIR SURPRISE

"**Y**es!" I cheered. "Our science fair project is up and ready to roll!"

"Awesome!" my twin sister, Ashley, said.

It was one day before the Orange Elementary School science fair. Kids from every grade were setting up their projects in the gym.

"Check it out, Mary-Kate," Ashley whispered to me. "Here comes the judge."

I glanced up from our exploding-volcano project. A man with gray hair and a large mustache was heading our way. It was Mr. Snyderbush—our science teacher and one of the judges for the science fair.

"Hello, Mary-Kate. Hello, Ashley," Mr. Snyderbush said. He pushed his wire-rimmed glasses up the bridge of his nose. "Is that an exploding volcano I see?"

"Not just any exploding volcano, Mr. Snyderbush!" I pointed out. "Our volcano spews stinky lava."

Mr. Snyderbush studied our volcano. It was molded out of papier-mâché with a small crater dug into the top. Hanging over it was a tiny glass bottle filled with our top secret stink formula.

"How stinky is it?" Mr. Snyderbush asked.

"Nine out of ten on the pee-ew scale!" Ashley answered.

"When real volcanoes spew, they smell like sulfur, the stuff that's in rotten eggs," I told Mr. Snyderbush. "So a stinky volcano is a realistic volcano!"

"That's absolutely correct!" Mr. Snyderbush said. "How did you get the idea for a superstinky volcano?"

Ashley squeezed her nose. "From our brother, Trent's, gym socks," she said.

"I see," Mr. Snyderbush said with a smile. "Keep up the good work, girls."

Ashley and I gave each other a high five as Mr. Snyderbush walked away.

"Our volcano is a hit, Ashley!" I exclaimed.

"Don't make room for that first-place trophy yet," Ashley warned. "We're up against some stiff competition."

"Really? Like what?" I asked.

Ashley pointed over my shoulder.

I whirled around. Two roller skates were whizzing by with *no feet* in them!

I gasped. "Whose experiment is that?"

"I'll give you two guesses." Ashley nodded in the direction of Dewey and Darcy Mills.

Dewey and Darcy were twins, just like

us! They were also the smartest kids in the fourth grade.

"How do you like our self-rolling roller skates?" Dewey asked as he and Darcy ran over to us. "All you do is put them on—and the skates do the rest."

"You can control them with this remote!" Darcy explained. She held up a small black box with an antenna sticking out of the top. Then she threw back her head and began to sneeze. "Ah-ahh-choo!"

"Gesundheit," Ashley and I said together.

"It's the hamster." Dewey sighed. He pointed to the hamster project at the table next to ours. "Darcy and I are allergic to fur."

"That's why we can't ever have a pet," Darcy said, sniffling.

"We just solved a case with mysterious sneezing in it," Ashley said. "'The Case of the Mall Mystery'!"

Ashley and I run the Olsen and Olsen

Detective Agency out of the attic of our house. We solve all kinds of mysteries.

"Pet allergies are a bummer," I said. "I couldn't imagine life without our dog, Clue!"

Clue was our silent partner. She helped us sniff out clues on lots of cases!

As the Mills twins ran back to their table, Ashley and I checked out the other projects. On the far side of the gym we found our friend Tim Park layering food in the shape of a pointy tower.

"Hey, Tim! What's that?" I asked.

"It's a food pyramid!" Tim explained. "It shows how to build a healthy diet by eating different kinds of food every day."

I smiled at Ashley. More than anything Tim loved to snack. No wonder his project was about food!

Ashley studied the chart next to Tim's pyramid. "This says that the bottom layer should be breads and cereals," she said. "You have jelly donuts there."

"They were easier to stack than cereal," Tim said. "And a lot tastier, too!"

"Don't get any ideas," I warned him. "You can't touch those donuts until after the science fair is over."

"I won't eat them!" Tim sighed. "It's those ants I'm worried about."

"Ants?" Ashley asked. "What ants?"

"The ants from Peter Belsky's ant farm," Tim said. He pointed to the table behind him.

Peter Belsky stood in front of a clear plastic tank filled with sand—and an army of hardworking ants.

Peter brushed some dirt off his sleeve. He was always messy. He spilled part of his lunch every day, and he was always being grounded for not cleaning his room.

"Cool project, Peter," I told him.

"Thanks. I'm just glad I got this ant farm here in one piece," Peter said. "Yesterday I dropped it and spilled sand and ants all over my room."

"If the ants escaped from the tank," Tim asked, "how did you find them all?"

"Luckily there was a three-day-old slice of pizza under my bed," Peter said, "and the ants headed right for it!"

"Yuck," Ashley said. She peered into the tank. "Why are those ants carrying cabbage leaves up that hill?" she asked.

"They're worker ants," Peter explained. Then he sighed. "I wish they'd work at cleaning my room."

Tim tugged my sleeve. "Hey," he said. "What's that?"

I looked in the direction Tim was pointing. In the corner stood a tall silver box big enough to stand up in. The box had a sign hanging on it that read: TREMENDOUS TIME MACHINE!

"Let's take a closer look," I told Ashley and Tim. The three of us hurried to the machine. We saw a door on one side of it. Next to the door was a lever that could be pointed to four different time periods: The Stone Age, the Roman Empire, the Middle Ages, and the 1800s.

Tim rubbed his hands together. "Let's take this baby for a test drive!" he said. "How about the Middle Ages?"

"Okay." I giggled. "But watch out for dragons!"

Tim turned the lever to the Middle Ages. The time machine began to tremble.

"Ouch!" a girl's voice muttered from behind the door. "I hate this stupid hat."

I stared at the time machine. The voice sounded familiar. And when the door swung open, I knew why.

Standing inside and wearing a long dress and a tall pointy hat was our friend Patty O'Leary!

"Welcome to the Middle Ages!" Patty declared. "When knights rode on horseback. And kings and queens reigned!"

"Not to mention princesses," Tim added.

I put a hand over my mouth to keep from laughing. Patty's nickname was Princess Patty because she usually got whatever she wanted.

"So, time travelers," Patty said, "what do you think of my science project?"

"You mean *history* project!" Tim said. "There's nothing scientific about it."

"So?" Patty asked. Her dress swished as she twirled. "If it was a plain old science project, I wouldn't get to wear costumes like this!"

"Hey, look over there!" someone shouted.

"I can't believe it!" another kid yelled.

Ashley and I turned. We saw kids and teachers charge to the other side of the gym.

"Where's everybody going?" Ashley hollered over the noise.

"I don't know," I shouted back. "But we'd better find out!"

2

DISAPPEARING DONUTS

Ashley, Tim, Patty, and I joined the crowd and ended up standing next to Dewey and Darcy.

"What's everyone looking at?" I asked. I stood on tiptoe, trying to see over the crowd's heads.

"Jessie Light's science project," Dewey explained. "It's some kind of robot."

"A robot?" Ashley asked. "No way!"

We squeezed our way to the front of the group. I saw our friend, Jessie Light, standing next to our principal, Mrs. Vega.

Then I saw what everyone was talking about—a silver robot sitting at a table behind a computer. He was about three feet tall and wore a red baseball cap with the word *Byte* on it.

The robot's head spun slowly. His eyes flashed, and his mouth flapped. "Hello," he said. "My name is Byte. I can write."

"Wow!" My jaw dropped as Byte began tapping the computer keys.

"E-mail document complete," Byte droned.

"Thank you, Byte," Jessie said. She turned the computer screen around so everyone could see Byte's e-mail.

"It says, 'Orange Elementary School rocks!'" a second-grade boy read out loud.

Everyone clapped and cheered.

"Does anyone have any questions about the robot for Jessie?" Mrs. Vega asked.

Ashley's hand shot up. "Can you tell us

a bit about how Byte works?" she asked.

Jessie opened a little door on Byte's back. Inside was a metal plate and bunches of colorful wires.

"This is Byte's memory system," Jessie explained. "All I have to do is repeat an action five times, and Byte learns it and repeats it."

"Can he do your homework?" Tim asked.

"He's not that smart!" Jessie chuckled. "But he does pack my backpack and make my lunch."

Everyone oohed and ahhed as Jessie pulled a peanut butter and jelly sandwich out of her backpack.

"It's perfect!" Tim swooned. "No drippy sides...no crusts. That sandwich is a masterpiece!"

"But I have to be careful," Jessie told us. "If I don't stop Byte, he'll repeat his actions over and over."

"Never-ending peanut butter and jelly

sandwiches?" Tim giggled. "That sounds good to me!"

Mr. Snyderbush pushed his way through the crowd. He clasped his hands together as he gazed at Byte.

"That robot is amazing!" Mr. Snyderbush shouted. "In fact, I've never seen one quite so incredible!"

"Thanks," Jessie said, beaming.

"You know," Mr. Snyderbush said slowly, "if I invented a robot like that, I'd win the Bowman Prize for sure!"

I gave Ashley a little nudge. Winning the famous Bowman Prize for Science was Mr. Snyderbush's dream. Everyone said he had his own secret lab, where he worked on his inventions every day after school.

"Does anyone else have any other questions?" Jessie asked with a smile.

Dewey raised his hand. "Does Byte come with instructions?" he asked.

Jessie unrolled a bluish sheet of paper.

"These are his plans," she said. "They show how to build Byte step by step."

"Why are they blue?" I asked.

"Most plans to build things are called blueprints," Jessie explained. "So I used lots of blue ink." She held up a thick blue marker.

Everyone crowded in to get a closer look at Byte.

"That robot is awesome!" a fourth-grade boy declared.

"The only robots I ever saw were in the movies," a girl from the third grade said. "And they can't make peanut butter and jelly sandwiches!"

Everyone seemed psyched about Byte. Well, almost everyone...

"It's not fair!" Patty muttered. She elbowed her way to the side of the gym, and grabbed one of Tim's jelly donuts.

"Hey, quit it!" Tim said as Patty bit into the donut. "You're going to knock over my whole pyramid!"

"Uh-oh," I whispered to Ashley. "Looks as if Patty is jealous of Jessie—and Byte."

Mrs. Vega clapped her hands for attention. "Okay, kids," she said. "Time to go to your classes."

"What about our science projects?" Ashley asked.

"Your projects will be locked in the gym until the science fair tomorrow," Mrs. Vega said. "Except for the hamster, of course."

As we filed out of the gym, I could hear Dewey and Darcy chatting about Byte.

"That robot rules!" Dewey said.

"Yeah!" Darcy agreed. "I wish we had one like him."

Who doesn't? I wondered. *Byte is really cool.*

We hurried to Room 202 and our science class. When we walked in, Mr. Snyderbush was pulling on his white lab coat. We watched as he slipped a pair of goggles over his eyes.

"Take your seats, boys and girls," Mr.

Snyderbush called out. "Today we are going to create cross-linked polymers."

"Huh?" Everyone gulped.

"In other words...we're going to make slime!" Mr. Snyderbush added.

Everyone cheered. Now *that* was more like it!

"But first"—Mr. Snyderbush turned to Jessie—"I want to know everything about Byte. And don't leave out a single detail."

"Well," Jessie began to explain, "my mom is an engineer. She found Byte in a Dumpster outside her lab."

"Really?" Mr. Snyderbush asked slowly.

Jessie nodded. "Mom and I took the robot in, and we programmed him to learn."

"Aha!" Patty shouted. "You had help with your science project. That's not fair!"

"What are you talking about?" Tim snapped. "Most kids had help from their parents. I bet *you* did, too."

"Yeah, well, I'm going to win that science fair," Patty grumbled. "Just you wait."

"All right, boys and girls," Mr. Snyderbush interrupted. "On with our experiment."

We gathered around the counter. Mr. Snyderbush mixed a white powder called borax and some water in a plastic bottle.

"Now remember," Mr. Snyderbush said, "never perform this experiment without an adult present."

Mr. Snyderbush placed some glue and some water into a cup. Then he swirled in a few drops of bright blue food coloring.

"Now I'm going to combine the two mixtures," Mr. Snyderbush said. "The result will be—"

"Slime!" Tim cheered. "Bring it on!"

Carefully Mr. Snyderbush combined the two mixtures in a large, clear container. Using a thin glass rod, he began to stir.

"Neat!" Dewey cried. "The liquid is turning into spongy stuff."

"That is the polymer, or slime," Mr. Snyderbush said excitedly.

I was pretty excited, too. Mr. Snyderbush stirred faster. The blue blob splashed out of the beaker, onto the floor—and all over Mr. Snyderbush's shoes.

"Eeeew! Gross!" Patty cried.

"Rats," Mr. Snyderbush muttered to himself. "When I win the Bowman Prize, there'll be no more silly school experiments for me!"

"Do you think the other kids will like our volcano at the fair tomorrow?" Ashley asked as we walked through the playground after school.

"Are you kidding? It's a total *blast*!" I joked.

Out of the corner of my eye I spotted Peter lugging a big black garbage bag over his shoulder.

"Hey, Peter!" I called. "What's in the bag?"

"My ant farm," Peter answered. "Mrs.

Vega told me I had to take it home."

"Why would she do that?" Ashley asked.

"Some of my ants escaped and ended up in the teachers' lounge." Peter sighed. "Mrs. Vega totally flipped out!"

Poor Peter! I thought. *He can never keep anything organized.*

"Oh, well," Peter said. "I'd better go straight home. I'm grounded for not cleaning my room."

"How can you stand being punished all the time?" I asked.

"It's not easy," Peter admitted. "I really have to turn over a new leaf."

"You mean you're going to try to be neat?" My voice squeaked.

Peter nodded.

"I'll believe that when I see it," Ashley whispered.

Peter smiled. "See you tomorrow!"

"'Bye!" I waved at Peter as he left the playground.

Ashley shook her head. "The day Peter cleans his room will be the day volcanoes spit snowballs."

"Now *that's* a cool idea for our next science project!" I declared.

Tuesday morning—the day of the science fair—Ashley and I practically ran to school. We were totally ready for the fair to begin. But when we walked into the gym, things didn't seem right.

"My food pyramid!" Tim cried out. "Someone ate my jelly donuts—and my whole pyramid caved in!"

I ran to Tim's table to check out the damage. Then—

"Oh, no!" Jessie shouted. "He's gone! My robot, Byte, is gone!"

3

BREAKING IN

"**W**hat's all the fuss about?" Mrs. Vega asked when she entered the gym.

"Mrs. Vega, my robot is missing!" Jessie cried. "I left him sitting at this table, and now he's gone. Even his blueprints have disappeared!"

"Hold on, Jessie. Maybe someone moved him," Ashley suggested. She turned to the principal. "Do you know if anyone came in here last night?"

Mrs. Vega shook her head. "I locked the

gym as soon as everyone was outside. No one was scheduled to be in here last night."

My head began to spin. What happened to Byte? Did someone take him?

"Okay, kids!" Mrs. Vega called out. "I want everybody to search the gym for Byte. Until he is found, this science fair will be postponed!"

Everyone gasped.

"Keep an eye out for loose computer chips, wires—" Mrs. Vega instructed.

"And raspberry jelly," Tim cried. "My donuts are missing, too!"

Ashley, Tim, and I peered behind the static-electricity experiments. We peeked under color charts. But we found no trace of Jesse's robot—or Tim's jelly donuts—anywhere.

I thought hard for a moment. "Hey, Jessie. If Byte can e-mail and make peanut butter and jelly sandwiches, do you think he could run away, too?"

"No," Jessie insisted. "Byte can only do what I taught him to do. Plus, once he's switched off, he can't do *anything*, and I made sure he was powered down before I left the gym yesterday."

"Then there's only one explanation," I said. "Somebody stole Byte!"

"And we've got a mystery to solve," Ashley finished.

Jessie reached into her pocket and pulled out a red plastic square with metal points stuck into one side of it.

"This is one of Byte's memory chips," Jessie explained. "I always keep a spare with me, in case Byte crashes. . . ."

She gave a little sniffle, then looked up at us. "I *have to* get Byte back. Do you think you can find Byte for me?"

"Absolutely!" I told Jessie.

"A missing robot is a perfect case for the Trenchcoat Twins!" Ashley declared.

"Wait a minute!" Tim cried. "My project

was ruined, too. Aren't you going to find out who stole my jelly donuts?"

I glanced at Ashley. She nodded.

"Sure, Tim," I said. "We'll take your case, too."

Tim sighed with relief. "Good. There's a donut thief out there. And he has to be stopped!" He turned and walked away.

"So, where should we start?" I asked my sister.

"Let's focus on Byte," Ashley suggested. "I have a feeling these two crimes are connected. Whoever took Byte could be the same person who swiped the donuts!"

"Good plan." I turned to Jessie and smiled. "Let's start with a list of suspects. Who would want to steal Byte?"

Ashley pulled out her detective pad and opened it to a fresh page. "How about Mr. Snyderbush?" she asked. "He said a robot like Byte could finally win him the Bowman Prize!"

"And he asked you tons of questions about Byte in science class," I told Jessie.

"You're right!" Jessie said, wide-eyed. "He *did* ask me a lot of questions."

Ashley wrote Mr. Snyderbush's name on her pad. It was hard to imagine our science teacher as a thief.

Who else would want to steal Byte? I thought.

My eyes darted around the gym. I spotted Patty standing next to her time machine. She was wearing a white top and a pink skirt with a red cherry design on it.

"Patty acted jealous of Byte," I pointed out. "And she did say she wanted to win the science fair, no matter what!"

"That's true," Ashley said. She added Patty's name to her list.

No other suspects came to mind, so we decided to question Patty first.

"Hi, Patty," Ashley called as we walked toward the time machine. I saw a big bandage on Patty's knee. I also noticed that the hem of her skirt was torn.

"Whoa! How did you skin your knee?" I asked.

"Um..." Patty glanced down. "I was climbing on the monkey bars."

"I thought monkey bars made you dizzy," Ashley said.

"They do!" Patty blurted. "That's why I slipped."

I watched as Patty edged closer and closer to the door of the time machine.

"Where were you yesterday after school?" Ashley asked.

"Why do you want to know?" Patty asked.

"Just curious," I told her.

"Well, I was at tap, gymnastics, tennis ...and Junior Brownie Chefs of America," she answered. She took a giant step to the side. Now she was totally blocking the door to the time machine!

That made me suspicious. Was there something behind the door that Patty didn't want us to see?

"Mind if we look *inside* your time machine?" I asked.

Patty blocked the door with her arms. "Yes, I do mind!" she snapped. "I've already called my father to come and pick up my project. I don't want anything bad to happen to it!"

Ashley tugged on my arm. "Come on, Mary-Kate. Let's go talk to someone else."

Together, we walked back to Jessie's table.

"Patty's guarding that time machine like a pit bull," Ashley reported to Jessie. "I think she's hiding something inside it."

"You mean like Byte?" Jessie asked.

"Maybe," Ashley said. She made note of it in her pad. "But we don't know for sure. We need to search the gym for more clues."

I rolled my eyes. Ashley and I may look

pretty much alike but we're different in one big way. When it comes to solving mysteries, I like to dive right in. But Ashley checks out each and every possibility *very* carefully.

Which is why she decided to look around one more time. And it's a good thing she did.

"Mary-Kate! Jessie!" Ashley exclaimed. "Look!"

She pointed to a window in the gym—an *open* window!

"The doors may have been locked last night," Ashley said, "but someone could have climbed in here."

I hurried over and checked out the windowsill. "Aha!" I said. "The dust here is smeared."

"What does that mean?" Jessie asked.

"It means someone disturbed it—probably when he or she was climbing through the window," I explained.

Then I noticed something else—a patch

of pink fabric stuck to the corner of the window frame.

The pink fabric had bright red cherries on it. I gasped. The material matched Patty's skirt!

Ashley grabbed the scrap of fabric. "Looks as if Patty didn't tear her skirt on the monkey bars after all."

"But this window is pretty high," Jessie pointed out. "How could Patty have reached it?"

"Good question!" I looked outside and saw a metal trash can on the ground underneath the window. "Patty must have used that for a boost."

"Princess Patty on a trash can?" Ashley chuckled. "She *must* have been desperate to get inside!"

"Maybe," I said. "But we won't know for sure until we sneak a peek inside that time machine!"

CAUGHT IN THE ACT

When the dismissal bell rang, Ashley and I ran straight home. As Ashley always says, even great detectives need a milk and cookie break.

After a few chocolate chip and oatmeal raisin cookies, we were ready for business.

"How are we going to peek inside that time machine?" Ashley asked as we headed out toward the O'Leary house. "What if Patty won't let us?"

I frowned. "Then we'll just have to be

extra sneaky about it, I guess," I told my sister.

We turned the corner onto Patty's street. I heard a weird rumbling noise followed by a loud, "Yee-haaaa!"

Ashley and I spun around. Whizzing down the block on a black-and-green skateboard was Peter Belsky!

"There's something you don't see every day," I told Ashley. "Peter playing outside after school."

"He must have cleaned his room." Ashley laughed.

"Where do you suppose Patty keeps the time machine?" I asked as we neared the O'Leary house.

"It's too big to keep in her room, so it's either in the backyard or the garage," Ashley guessed.

HMMMMMMMMM.

Ashley and I jumped back. Patty's garage door was opening!

Mrs. O'Leary drove the car out of the garage. I saw Patty, sitting in the front seat, wearing a pink leotard. We waved, but Patty didn't see us.

"Ballet!" I wailed. "I forgot that Patty has ballet on Tuesdays."

"Mrs. O'Leary must be in a hurry. She forgot to close the garage door!" Ashley said. As the car backed out of the driveway, I peeked into the garage. I saw something silvery inside. I took a step closer. Yes! It was the time machine.

"Ashley! Come on, let's look inside it," I called.

We raced straight to Patty's project. I pulled at the handle, but the door wouldn't budge.

"The lever!" Ashley remembered. "We have to turn the lever to a time in history!"

Right! I turned the lever all the way back to the Stone Age. Then I grabbed the handle again. This time the door began to open.

I peered inside the time machine.

"What's in there, Mary-Kate?" Ashley asked.

There were costumes hanging everywhere. I noticed Patty's pointy hat—the one she wore the other day—dangling from a hook. It was dripping with sticky red goo!

I stepped inside the time machine—and my shoe stuck to the floor. I glanced down and saw more goo on floor of the time machine.

"Eww!" Ashley said as she looked over my shoulder. "What is that?"

"I don't know." I reached out and touched the goo on Patty's hat. It was kind of lumpy and very sticky.

"I think it's…jelly!" I said. I took a whiff. "It smells like raspberry jelly!"

Ashley gasped. "Tim's donuts were filled with raspberry jelly. That means Patty could be the donut thief!"

"And the robot thief," I pointed out.

"Come on," Ashley said. "Let's search some more before Patty comes back and—"

"Before *what*?" a voice interrupted.

I turned and gasped. Patty was standing right behind us. And she looked mad!

"Patty!" Ashley cried. "What are you doing here?"

"I came back for my ballet scrunchie," Patty snapped. "What are *you* doing here?"

I held up a finger—the one with the jelly on it. "We know what you did, Patty."

Ashley pulled the pink, cherry-patterned fabric from her pocket.

"Where did you find that?" Patty gasped.

"It was hanging on the gym windowsill," Ashley answered. "We know you were in the gym when you weren't supposed to be. It's time to tell us the truth!"

"All right, all right," Patty said. "You caught me. I did it!"

5

A COMPUTER CLUE

*Y*es! I thought, smiling my biggest smile ever. *We found the thief in record time! Jessie will be so happy to get Byte back. And everyone will be happy that the science fair is back on!*

"Why don't you tell us the whole story, Patty," Ashley said. "From the beginning."

Patty stared at the goo inside the time machine.

Then she heaved a big sigh. "Okay, fine," she said. "I *did* climb into the gym before school started this morning."

"To take Byte?" I asked, folding my arms.

"No way!" Patty said. "I wanted to type *I'm a cheater* on Byte's computer screen. Because Jessie had help with her project."

"So what happened?" Ashley asked.

"When I made it into the gym, Byte was already gone," Patty said. "I was so upset, I decided to take a few jelly donuts from Tim's food pyramid.

"The whole pyramid started to tumble," Patty went on. "I got scared that someone might have heard the crash. So I hid inside my time machine with the donuts. I bit into a big fat donut, and jelly squirted everywhere! Then I accidentally dropped another two, and they oozed all over the floor. When I was sure no one was around, I sneaked back outside."

"So *that's* why you wouldn't let us into your time machine?" I asked Patty.

"Exactly," Patty said. "If I did, everyone

would know I stole Tim's jelly donuts."

"And you really didn't take Jessie's robot?" Ashley asked.

"No way!" Patty insisted. "I didn't steal Byte. I just took a few donuts, that's all."

I stared hard at Patty. Could she be lying? No, I decided. She was telling the truth.

The honk of a car horn made us jump.

"That's my mom," Patty said. "I'd better get my scrunchie and go."

"Wait!" Ashley said. "Do you promise to replace Tim's donuts?"

"What for?" Patty asked. "There's never going to be a science fair. Mrs. Vega is going to cancel it because that dumb robot is missing."

"There *is* going to be a science fair," I said. "The Trenchcoat Twins will not give up until we find Byte!"

That night Ashley and I sat on the floor of Jessie's room, updating her about the case.

"At least we know who took Tim's jelly donuts," Ashley said.

"But we still haven't found Byte," I pointed out.

Ashley opened her detective notebook. "We need to move on to another suspect."

"The only suspect left is Mr. Snyderbush," Jessie said.

"What do we know about him so far?" Ashley asked.

"We know that Mr. Snyderbush wants to win the Bowman Prize," Jessie said. "Really badly!"

"And that he has a secret lab," I added. "Maybe we could search it. Does anyone know where it is?"

"If we did, it wouldn't be secret!" Ashley told us.

"I know where Mr. Snyderbush lives," Jessie said. "Somewhere on Neutron Street."

I giggled. Even his address sounded scientific!

"Hmm." Ashley thought out loud. "What if his secret lab is somewhere inside his house?"

"Then we can look through his windows for Byte," I suggested. "As Great-grandma Olive always says, '*Peek* and you shall find!'"

"Is your great-grandmother a detective, too?" Jessie asked, surprised.

"The best!" Ashley declared. "Great-grandma Olive used to read mystery books to Mary-Kate and me when we were little."

"Until we decided to solve some mysteries of our own," I added. "Just like this one!"

We were interrupted by a voice on Jessie's computer. She had e-mail!

Ashley and I followed Jessie to her computer. We looked over her shoulder as she clicked the mouse. The message was from someone named SLOTH.

"I don't know anyone with that address," Jessie said.

"Open up the message," I urged Jessie.

Jessie clicked, and the e-mail message appeared: *Orange Elementary School rocks!*

Jessie gasped. "I-I can't believe it!"

"What is it?" Ashley asked.

"It's a message from Byte!" Jessie answered.

"How do you know?" I asked.

"Because I taught him to type that message. I taught him how to send e-mail!" Jessie said.

"Then it's not just a message," I told her. "It's a clue!"

6

THE SECRET LAB

"**H**uh? How is this e-mail a clue?" Jessie asked.

"If Byte can send you e-mail, we know that he's somewhere near a computer," I told her.

"And whoever has him uses the e-mail address SLOTH," Ashley added. "If we find SLOTH, we have our thief!"

We used Jessie's e-mail program to do a profile check on the address SLOTH. It was a dead end. No one with that address had entered a profile.

Jessie printed out the message and gave it to me as evidence. Then Ashley and I got ready to leave.

"Don't worry, Jessie," I said. "We solved Tim's case. And now we'll solve yours."

The next morning Ashley and I met Jessie in the school yard.

"Look," Jessie said. She handed Ashley a piece of paper. "I got another e-mail from SLOTH this morning."

Ashley scrunched her eyebrows as she studied the message. Just like the first one, it read: *Orange Elementary School rocks!*

I laughed. "Boy, Byte must really like our school."

"That's the only message Byte knows how to type," Jessie explained.

I wanted to help Jessie find Byte. I wanted to save the school science fair. And I wanted to do it right now! But we couldn't. Instead we would have to wait until after school to check out Mr. Snyderbush's house.

"Wait a minute. What if Mr. Snyderbush is at home after school?" I asked. "It will be much harder to snoop around then."

"He won't be," Jessie said. "There's a special teachers' conference today. Mr. Snyderbush will have to stay after school."

We exchanged high fives. The three of us were turning out to be a pretty good team!

As we walked through the school yard, I saw a small crowd of kids on the basketball court. Instead of shooting hoops, they were watching Darcy jump rope!

"Hi!" Dewey called to us. "Check out our special state-of-the-art jump rope."

"What makes it special?" I called back.

"The handles contain computerized counters," Darcy shouted as she hopped. "They keep track of your jumps. They can even tell you how fast you're jumping!"

Darcy began jumping faster and faster. Everything in her pockets began to fly out!

"Whoops," Darcy muttered.

Ashley, Jessie, and I ran to help Darcy pick up her stuff. There was a digital pen, a pack of gum called CyberBubbles, and—

"What are these?" Ashley asked. She scooped up three computer chips. Three *red* computer chips!

"I'll take those!" Dewey said. He grabbed the chips from Ashley just as the school bell rang.

"Thanks for helping," Darcy said quickly. She crammed her stuff back into her pockets. Then she and Dewey ran off.

"Did you see those chips?" Jessie asked. "They looked just like Byte's!"

"Hmm." I thought out loud. "Dewey and Darcy did say they wanted a robot like Byte!"

"So did most of the kids in school," Ashley said. "And Dewey grabbed those chips before we got a close enough look. We need more—"

"—evidence!" I finished. "I know, I know.

But we should definitely add Dewey and Darcy to our list of suspects!"

The bell rang again, and the three of us lined up at the school door with the rest of the kids.

Jessie began sniffing the air. "I smell peanut butter," she said.

"Must be my lunch!" a voice piped up.

I turned and saw Peter Belsky standing behind us. He smiled as he opened up his backpack. "See? One peanut butter and jelly sandwich."

The line began to move. I could see tears in Jessie's eyes.

"Peanut butter and jelly!" She sighed. "Just like Byte used to make!"

"Don't worry, Jessie," I said, patting her shoulder. "We'll find Byte. I promise."

"No milk and cookie break for us today?" Ashley asked.

I shook my head. "Not today," I said. "We

have to make it to Mr. Snyderbush's house before the teachers' conference ends."

Ashley, Jessie, and I reached Neutron Street in under ten minutes. It wasn't hard to tell which house was Mr. Snyderbush's. It was the one with the talking mailbox!

"You've got mail! You've got mail!" the box repeated.

I watched the little red flag on the mailbox move up and down. "Mr. Snyderbush thinks of everything!" I said.

We walked up the path to Mr. Snyderbush's house. It looked pretty normal from the outside.

"Where could his secret lab be?" I asked.

"Mad scientists usually keep them up in a tower," Ashley said.

"Except this house is one level," Jessie pointed out.

We tried to peek through all the windows. No luck. Each one had thick drapes hanging inside.

"Shh!" Ashley said. She put a finger to her lips. "Did you hear that?"

WHIRRRRR...WHIRRRRR!

"That noise!" Jessie said excitedly. "It's the same noise that Byte makes!"

"But where is it coming from?" Ashley asked.

We followed the noise around the house—right to a cellar door in the ground.

"Byte is down there. I just know it." Jessie shuddered. "We have to rescue him!"

I grabbed the handle on the cellar door. The door creaked as I yanked it open.

Ashley climbed down a few stairs. The cellar was pretty dark. And creepy!

"What do you see in there?" I called after Ashley.

CRASH! Something shattered in the darkness.

"Mary-Kate! Jessie!" Ashley shouted. "Come down here. Hurry!"

GUILTY AS CHARGED

Jessie and I charged down the stairs. "Ashley! What is it?"

"See for yourself!" Ashley flipped on a light. I glanced around. The cellar was filled with beakers, Bunsen burners, bubbling test tubes, microscopes, and flickering computer screens. One of the beakers lay broken on the floor. Ashley must have bumped into it in the dark.

"It's the secret lab!" I declared.

WHIRRR...WHIRRR!

"Byte?" Jessie called. "Byte, is that you?"

The sound grew louder. And louder.

Then a robot appeared from the shadows!

"Hello," the robot droned. His eyes flashed and his arms jerked. "My name is Dennis. Anyone for tennis?"

"That's not Byte!" Jessie shouted.

"No kidding!" I yelped as the robot picked up a tennis racket.

"Your serve, your serve," Dennis said. He walked toward us, swinging his racket back and forth.

"Look out!" Ashley said.

CRASH! CRUNCH!

I flinched as Dennis knocked over beakers and test tubes.

"He's out of control!" Jessie cried.

We backed against a wall and covered our faces. Dennis continued to swing, inching closer and closer.

I heard the thunder of footsteps.

"Dennis!" a voice cried. "Drop that now!"

I peeked out between my fingers. It was Mr. Snyderbush, holding a remote!

"Shoddy parts!" Mr. Snyderbush muttered as he clicked the remote. "I suppose you get what you pay for."

The whirring stopped. Dennis froze with the tennis racket in the air.

"What are you girls doing in my lab?" Mr. Snyderbush demanded. "You could have been hurt."

"We were looking for Byte," Ashley spoke up. "We heard you say that you could win the Bowman Prize if you had him—and then he disappeared!"

"Mr. Snyderbush, did you sneak into the gym the day Byte was stolen?" I asked.

Mr. Snyderbush's mustache began to twitch. "All right, girls. All right—you caught me."

CLUE FINDS A CLUE

Jessie blinked. "You mean, you really *did* take Byte?"

Mr. Snyderbush coughed. "Now wait a minute! I would never do that. Never."

I frowned. "But you just said that—"

"I said that you caught me," Mr. Snyderbush said. "And you're right, I did sneak into the gym. But not to steal Byte."

"Then why?" I asked.

"I wanted to look *inside* Byte," Mr. Snyderbush explained. "To see exactly how he was programmed. I've been working on Dennis for years but I wasn't sure how to make one of his connections work. Once I checked Byte's memory system, I found the answer to my problem."

Dennis gave another whir. He dropped his tennis racket with a clang.

"Well...almost." Mr. Snyderbush sighed. Then he went on. "I really wanted that Bowman Prize. And...a decent tennis partner."

Mr. Snyderbush sure sounded as if he was telling the truth, but I still had to ask him one last thing. "Mr. Snyderbush, do you have your own e-mail address?"

"Why, of course," Mr. Snyderbush answered. "It's WEIRDSCIENCE. Why?"

I frowned. "No reason."

Mr. Snyderbush smiled at each of us. "Girls, I hope you understand that I would never steal Byte," he said. "And I do hope you find him."

So did we! We thanked Mr. Snyderbush.

Then we climbed out of the secret lab.

"So what do we do now?" Jessie asked.

"We've got two more suspects," Ashley said. "Dewey and Darcy Mills."

"Let's go see them," I suggested. "But first we need to get home. It's time to walk our silent partner, Clue!"

"Who?" Jessie asked.

"Our basset hound," Ashley explained. "Her nose may be cold, but it's always hot on the trail for clues!"

We raced home to introduce Jessie to our dog. Clue's long ears bounced as she ran out to greet us.

"Let Clue sniff you, Jessie." Ashley snapped Clue's leash onto her collar. "That's how dogs get to know people."

"Okay," Jessie said. She kneeled down, placing her backpack on the ground.

Clue nuzzled her nose into Jessie's palm. She gave a few quick sniffs. Then she moved over to the backpack. She started snorting wildly and wagging her tail.

"What is it, girl?" I asked. "What do you smell?"

Jessie reached into the backpack and pulled out her fat blue marker—the one she used to make Byte's blueprints. "I think she likes this," Jessie said.

"Woof!" Clue barked. She smelled the marker some more.

"That's enough sniffing, Clue!" Ashley said. "We have work to do."

Jessie put the marker into her pencil case. The four of us walked toward Dewey and Darcy's house.

We turned onto their street, and Clue froze in place. She began sniffing the air.

"WOOF!" She kicked up her hind legs and took off like a rocket!

"What happened?" Jessie asked.

Ashley smiled as Clue tugged her along. "I think that Clue just sniffed a clue!"

9

SNIFFING OUT
THE SUSPECTS

"**C**lue!" I called as we followed Ashley down the street. "Slow down!"

But Clue was hot on the trail. For what, we didn't know. But we were sure going to find out!

I could see two kids walking halfway up the block.

"Look! It's Dewey and Darcy!" Ashley called back to us.

"Woof!" Clue barked.

The Mills twins turned around.

"Ahhh!" Darcy yelled, staring at Clue.

"Ahhh!" Dewey yelled, too. "Allergies! Let's get out of here!"

The two began to run. Darcy's red backpack bounced up and down behind her.

Dewey and Darcy turned into the driveway of their house.

"Ah-choo!" Darcy tripped and fell onto the lawn. Her backpack spilled open onto the ground.

Clue sniffed Darcy's things like crazy.

"Get away!" Darcy shouted.

"Clue!" Ashley scolded. "How rude!"

I was about to help Darcy collect her stuff, when I saw Clue sniffing a bright blue scroll.

"Wait a minute. This looks familiar," Jessie said. She picked up the scroll and unrolled it. "Look! Its Byte's blueprints! They fell from Darcy's backpack!"

"No way!" I gasped and looked down at our dog. "Clue, how did you—?"

"I think I know," Ashley said. "Clue liked the smell of the ink from Jessie's marker. She smelled it again when she got near Darcy's backpack!"

"Good girl, Clue!" I cried. "You found a thief!"

Clue grunted. She rolled onto her back for a belly rub.

"Okay, you two," Ashley said, staring hard at Darcy and Dewey. "What are you doing with Byte's blueprints?"

Dewey and Darcy held up their hands.

"We're sorry!" Darcy said. "You caught us! We did it!"

10

A CHANGE OF PLANS

"Ah-chooo!" Darcy sneezed again.

Honk! Dewey blew his nose into some tissues. "Keep that dog away from us," he begged. "We're allergic to fur, you know."

I held up Byte's blueprints. "Allergies explain your sneezing. But how do you explain this?"

"Darcy and I were the last to leave the gym on Monday," Dewey explained. "So on our way out, we snatched Byte's plans."

"We were going to put them back on

Jessie's porch, when your dog charged us!" Darcy said.

"If you have the blueprints," Jessie said excitedly, "you must have Byte, too!"

Dewey and Darcy shook their heads.

"We didn't take Byte!" Darcy insisted. "Just the plans."

I groaned. Not again! It seemed as if everyone was confessing, but no one had stolen Byte!

"If you don't have Byte, then why were you carrying around those red computer chips?" I asked. "They were the same as the ones Jessie said she used in Byte."

Dewey pulled a remote from his jacket pocket. He held it toward the yard and gave it a click.

I heard a bark. A shiny silver dog tramped out from behind a tree.

"Woof! Woof!" the dog barked. "My name is Jelly. Would you scratch my belly?"

I stared as the dog's head whirled

around in a complete circle. His orange eyes flashed on and off, and his metallic ears spun like pinwheels.

"We could never have a real dog," Dewey explained. "So we decided to build a robotic dog!"

"We never planned to build a robot until we saw Byte," Dewey admitted. "Seeing him gave us the idea to build Jelly."

Clue sniffed Jelly's metal nose. She whined when Jelly turned his head in a full circle.

"Woof! Woof!" Jelly said. "I'm glad you're here. Will you scratch my ear?"

Jessie patted Jelly on his hard head. Her pats made loud thunking sounds.

"We have loads of computer chips at home," Dewey explained. "And now you see why."

Dewey turned to Jessie. "We're really sorry we took Byte's blueprints," he said. "But we knew they could help us create a pet. And we just wanted one so badly…"

"Apology accepted." Jessie smiled. "I guess if you can't have a real dog, a robo-dog is the next best thing."

"And Jelly is just like a real dog!" I added.

"That's for sure!" Darcy giggled. "He even drinks out of the toilet."

"Woof!" Jelly barked.

I remembered Byte's e-mail—the one from the strange address, SLOTH.

"One last thing," I said. "Do you guys have e-mail addresses?"

"We share one," Darcy told us. "It's TWIN2TWIN."

"Oh. Thanks." I sighed.

Ashley, Jessie, and I waved good-bye to the Mills twins. Then we left their yard.

"Now we have zero suspects!" Jessie wailed. "Do you think we should just give up?"

"Give up?" Ashley cried. "No way!"

"Our Great-grandma Olive never gives up," I declared. "And neither do we!"

Jessie smiled. I think that's exactly what she wanted to hear!

"Are you sure this is the same window?" Ashley asked.

I nodded. "Absolutely. The trash can is still underneath it."

It was Thursday afternoon. Ashley, Jessie, and I were in the school yard after class, looking for clues. This time we searched *outside* the gym window.

I lifted the lid off the trash can. Inside was a clear plastic tank.

"That looks just like the tank Peter's ant farm was in," Jessie observed.

"That's weird," I said. "I thought Peter was carrying his ant farm home on Monday."

"Hold on a minute. If Peter didn't take his ant farm home," Ashley said, "then what do you think he was carrying in that trash bag?"

"Maybe *he* took Byte!" Jessie said.

"Hey, you guys! Guess what?" Tim called as he ran over to us. "Mrs. Vega wants us to take our science projects home. The science fair is cancelled until further notice."

"Cancelled?" Ashley cried.

"Yeah. Because nobody returned Byte yet," Tim replied.

"Rats," I grumbled. "We should have solved this case by now. And saved the science fair."

Ashley put a hand on my shoulder. "Come on, Mary-Kate. We've got one more lead to follow. Let's go!"

"I know Peter lives on Blueberry Lane," I said. "But I don't know his address."

"Let's walk around and check out the mailboxes for his name," Ashley suggested.

We walked with Jessie up and down Blueberry Lane, but we couldn't find Peter's house anywhere.

We were about to stop looking when—

"Beep, beep!" a voice yelled.

I looked up the block and saw a five-year-old boy pedaling a tricycle. He had light blond hair, covered by a red baseball cap.

Wait a minute. That red cap...

The boy turned. The cap had Byte's name on it!

"Ashley! Jessie!" I called out. "Follow that kid!"

11

COMING CLEAN

"**T**hat little boy is wearing Byte's baseball cap," I explained to Ashley and Jessie. "Maybe he knows where Byte is!"

We ran up to the boy. "Hi there!" I called. "What's your name?"

The boy smiled. "I'm Adam."

"Hi, Adam. I'm Ashley. This is my sister, Mary-Kate, and my friend Jessie. We really like your baseball cap," Ashley said. "I want one just like it. Where did you get it?"

"I found it," Adam said, shrugging.

"Where did you find it?" Jessie asked.

"By my house," Adam answered.

"Do you think you could show me where your house is?" I asked.

"Sure," Adam told us.

He led us to a mint-colored house on Blueberry Lane. It was one level with dark green shutters and a roof to match.

The house's front door swung open. Peter Belsky stepped out, dressed for karate. He froze when he saw us.

"That's my brother!" Adam said.

"H-hi, guys," Peter stammered.

I folded my arms across my chest. "Hi, Peter. We just met your brother. He's got a really nice cap."

"Uh, yeah. I don't know where got it," Peter said.

"He probably got it from Byte, since it has Byte's name on it," Jessie said. "Where is he? Where is Byte?"

Peter stared at us. "Beats me. Why would

I know anything about Byte?" he asked.

CLUNK!

A potted plant fell from the windowsill and onto the walkway.

"Klutzy robot," Peter muttered.

I stared at Peter. "Did you just say 'klutzy *robot*'?"

"Peter has a robot in his room," Adam piped up. "Want to see him? Follow me!"

Adam marched right past Peter and in the front door.

Ashley, Jessie, and I raced inside the house.

"Hey!" Peter yelped. "You can't do that! Come back!"

I glanced around and noticed a long hall-way. There was a door at the end of it, with a sign that read: KEEP OUT!

"That's Peter's room," Adam said.

"No! Don't go in there!" Peter yelled.

Adam quickly grabbed the knob and pushed open the door. Ashley, Jessie, and I stepped into the room and looked around.

There, wearing an apron and carrying a broom—was Byte!

"Don't forget the dust bunnies!" Byte droned as he swept the floor. "Sweep, sweep, sweep!"

"Byte!" Jessie cried happily. "You're safe!"

Ashley and I turned to Peter. Beads of sweat dotted his forehead.

"I-I..." Peter stammered.

I glanced around and noticed that Peter had a computer in his room. I grabbed the mouse and clicked onto Peter's e-mail program.

Aha! Just as I suspected! Peter's screen name was SLOTH.

I pointed at Peter. "It was you! You stole Byte! You've had him since Monday, and you never said a word to anyone!"

"Stealing Byte was totally terrible, Peter," Ashley said. "Why did you do it?"

Peter sighed. "I guess I better explain. . . ."

A First Prize Team

"**I** was sick of being grounded," Peter said. "But I kept forgetting to clean my room. So when I saw Byte, I had a brainstorm. If I had Byte, I could get him to do the cleaning."

"Don't forget to polish the doorknobs!" Byte interrupted. "Buff, buff, buff!"

"Mrs. Vega told me to take my ant farm home after some ants ended up in the teachers' lounge. She let me into the gym and waited outside for me to get my project."

"Why did she wait outside?" Ashley asked.

Peter shrugged. "She was so grossed out when the ants crawled up her leg that she didn't want to go near them."

"What happened next?" I asked.

"I saw Byte sitting there, and I knew I had to have him," Peter went on. "I opened the gym window and dumped the dirt from my ant farm onto the ground to set the ants free. Then I dropped the tank into the open trash can underneath."

That explains the trashed tank we found, I thought. *And the open window!*

"Then you stashed Byte in the bag and made everyone think it was your ant farm," Ashley said.

"You got it." Peter sighed. He turned to Jessie. "I hope you're not too mad. I just didn't want to be punished anymore."

Jessie sighed. "Well, a couple of good things came out of all this."

"Like what?" Ashley and I asked together.

"I got Byte back." Jessie smiled. "And

now he really knows how to clean a ro

"Thanks to me." Peter groaned. "I had to clean my room five times before he got the hang of it."

"And speaking of clean..." Ashley told Peter. "It's time *you* came clean. You have to tell Mrs. Vega and Mr. Snyderbush what you did."

Peter covered his face with his hands. "I was afraid you'd say that!"

"Clean, clean, clean," Byte chimed in. "Don't forget under the rug!"

I laughed as Byte shook a dusty rag out the window. I was so happy, I wanted to burst. Jessie had Byte back. We solved another case. And last but not least, we saved the Orange Elementary School science fair!

"Okay, boys and girls!" Mrs. Vega called out on Monday morning. "You've all demonstrated your science projects. And ow it's time for the judges to make their decisions."

Ashley and I squeezed hands behind our volcano. Our project spewed and stank without a hitch!

"No way will I win!" Tim whispered.

I turned toward him. He was standing next to his food pyramid, looking pretty bummed out. "Why not?" I asked.

"The whole bottom layer is missing," he told us.

"But I thought Patty replaced all your jelly donuts," Ashley said.

"She did!" Tim told us. "But this time I couldn't resist. I ate all of the donuts by *myself*!"

I laughed. "You think *you* have problems! For taking Byte, Peter Belsky has to clean our classroom after school every day for the whole year. He even has to scrub the hamster cage!"

Ashley and I both felt bad for Peter. But

we also knew that he got what he deserved. As Great-grandma Olive likes to say, "The punishment must fit the crime!"

Mr. Snyderbush stepped to the front of the gym, holding a metal clipboard. "And now, boys and girls," he said, clearing his throat, "the first prize goes to—Jessie Light and her robot, Byte!"

"Yes!" I cheered. Ashley and I jumped up and down. Even if we didn't win, we were glad Jessie did!

Everyone clapped as Jessie received her blue ribbon. She pinned it on Byte's cap. Then she ran over to us.

"Thanks, you guys!" Jessie said, her eyes shining. "I couldn't have done it without your help."

I shook my head and grinned. "Byte was your brainstorm, Jessie," I said. "You deserve every inch of that blue ribbon."

"You deserve a prize, too!" Jessie told us.

"You mean for inventing the stinkiest

volcano ever?" Ashley asked.

Jessie shook her head.

"For solving this case," she said. "You two definitely have detective work down— to a science!"

Hi from both of us,

When Ashley and I arrived at Camp Crooked Lake this summer, we were ready for hours of swimming, canoeing, and waterskiing fun.

But we didn't know that the camp had a terrible secret—and that when we stepped off of our bus, were we stepping right into a mystery—our most dangerous mystery yet!

Want to find out more? Turn the page for a sneak peek at *The New Adventures of Mary-Kate & Ashley: The Case Of Camp Crooked Lake.*

See you next time!

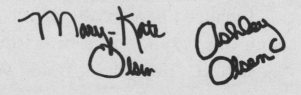

A sneak peek at our next mystery…

The Case Of
CAMP CROOKED LAKE

Our first cookout at Camp Crooked Lake was totally awesome! Joy, one of the junior counselors, handed out hotdogs and sticks to all the campers. Ashley and I roasted the dogs ourselves over the big bonfire. They were delicious!

After we ate, a senior counselor named Steve wanted to tell ghost stories.

"Why don't we roast some marshmallows while you're scaring us?" I asked.

"Good idea," Steve said.

I glanced over at the picnic table. Vicki, one our cabin mates, was standing right next to it. "Hey, Vicki! Could you toss that bag of marshmallows over here, please?"

With a sigh, Vicki picked up the bag and threw it to me. "Thanks!" I said. I untwisted the plastic tie and reached into the bag. "Oh, gross!" I cried. I dropped the bag and wiped my hand on my jeans. "There are bugs in there!"

"No kidding?" Steve picked up the bag and looked inside. "Hey, Mary-Kate's right. These marshmallows are crawling with insects."

"That's disgusting!" Ashley said.

The senior counselors exchanged glances. "It's starting, isn't it?" a counselor named April asked.

"What do you mean?" I asked nervously. "What's starting?"

"It's the curse," April replied, "the Curse of Camp Crooked Lake! We're all doomed!"

It's a countdown to
the biggest party of the year!
Take a sneak peek at what's
happening in

BOOK 1: *Never Been Kissed*

I sat on the park bench, staring at Jake Impenna, the coolest, nicest guy in Bayside High School. Our afternoon date had been totally fun. So much fun that I couldn't wait for him to ask me out again.

"So, have I locked in an invitation to your big sweet sixteen party yet?" Jake asked, giving me a wide smile.

All the blood rushed out of my face. Ashley and I had been planning our sweet sixteen party for weeks. It was supposed to be the most important night of our lives. How could I explain that Ashley wanted an all-girl party? How could I tell Jake that he wasn't invited?

Think, Mary-Kate! I told myself. Think!

"Yeah," I said finally. "I mean...yes, of course you're invited."

"Excellent," Jake said. His gray eyes twinkled.

My heart thudded against my ribcage. So I'd gone with my heart. So what? I would just have to get Ashley to change her mind about inviting boys.

I knew I could do it. It would be absolutely no problem. Right?

WIN a MARY-KATE and ASHLEY Around the World Prize Pack!

Enter below for your chance to win great prizes including:

- A set of autographed books including *Our Lips are Sealed, Winning London, Holiday in the Sun* and *Passport to Paris Scrapbook*

- A video library including *Passport to Paris, Our Lips are Sealed, Winning London, Holiday in the Sun* and *You're Invited to Mary-Kate and Ashley's Vacation Parties*

- A *Mary-Kate and Ashley Travel in Style* doll giftset

You'll even get a personal phone call from Mary-Kate and Ashley!

THE NEW ADVENTURES OF MARY-KATE & ASHLEY™

Mary-Kate and Ashley Around the World Prize Pack Sweepstakes

OFFICIAL RULES:

1. No purchase necessary.

2. To enter complete the official entry form or hand print your name, address, age, and phone number along with the words "THE NEW ADVENTURES OF MARY-KATE & ASHLEY Around the World Prize Pack Sweepstakes" on a 3" x 5" card and mail to: THE NEW ADVENTURES OF MARY KATE & ASHLEY Around the World Prize Pack Sweepstakes, c/o HarperEntertainment, Attn: Children's Marketing Department, 10 East 53rd Street, New York, NY 10022, entries must be received **no later than July 31, 2002.** Enter as often as you wish, but each entry must be mailed separately. One entry per envelope. Partially completed, illegible, or mechanically reproduced entries will not be accepted. Sponsors are not responsible for lost, late, mutilated, illegible, stolen, postage due, incomplete, or misdirected entries. All entries become the property of Dualstar Entertainment Group, Inc., and will not be returned.

3. Sweepstakes open to all legal residents of the United States, (excluding Colorado and Rhode Island), who are between the ages of five and fifteen on July 31, 2002, excluding employees and immediate family members of HarperCollins Publishers, Inc. ("HarperCollins"), Parachute Properties and Parachute Press, Inc., and their respective subsidiaries and affiliates, officers, directors, shareholders, employees, agents, attorneys, and other representatives (individually and collectively "Parachute"), Dualstar Entertainment Group, Inc., and its subsidiaries and affiliates, officers, directors, shareholders, employees, agents, attorneys, and other representatives (individually and collectively "Dualstar"), and their respective parent companies, affiliates, subsidiaries, advertising, promotion and fulfillment agencies, and the persons with whom each of the above are domiciled. Offer void where prohibited or restricted by law.

4. Odds of winning depend on the total number of entries received. Approximately 450,000 sweepstakes notices distributed. Prize will be awarded. Winner will be randomly drawn on or about August 15, 2002, by HarperCollins Publishers Inc., whose decisions are final. Potential winner will be notified by mail and will be required to sign and return an affidavit of eligibility and release of liability within 14 days of notification. Prize won by minor will be awarded to parent or legal guardian who must sign and return all required legal documents. By acceptance of the prize, winner consents to the use of his or her name, photograph, likeness, and personal information by HarperCollins, Parachute, Dualstar, and for publicity purposes without further compensation except where prohibited.

5. One (1) Grand Prize Winner wins a Mary-Kate and Ashley Around the World Prize Pack, consisting of the following: a set of autographed books including PASSPORT TO PARIS SCRAPBOOK, OUR LIPS ARE SEALED, WINNING LONDON, HOLIDAY IN THE SUN ; a set of videos including PASSPORT TO PARIS, OUR LIPS ARE SEALED, WINNING LONDON, HOLIDAY IN THE SUN, and YOU'RE INVITED TO MARY-KATE AND ASHLEY'S VACATION PARTIES; a MARY-KATE AND ASHLEY TRAVEL IN STYLE doll giftset; a Mary-Kate and Ashley sunblock; a 10 minute phone call from Mary-Kate and Ashley (subject to availability). Approximate retail value: $165.

6. Only one prize will be awarded per individual, family, or household. Prize is non-transferable and cannot be sold or redeemed for cash. No cash substitute is available. Any federal, state, or local taxes are the responsibility of the winner. Sponsor may substitute prize of equal or greater value, if necessary, due to availability.

7. Additional terms: By participating, entrants agree a) to the official rules and decisions of the judges, which will be final in all respects; and to waive any claim to ambiguity of the official rules and b) to release, discharge, and hold harmless HarperCollins, Parachute, Dualstar, and their affiliates, subsidiaries, and advertising and promotion agencies from and against any and all liability or damages associated with acceptance, use, or misuse of any prize received in this sweepstakes.

8. Any dispute arising from this Sweepstakes will be determined according to the laws of the State of New York, without reference to its conflict of law principles, and the entrants consent to the personal jurisdiction of the State and Federal courts located in New York County and agree that such courts have exclusive jurisdiction over all such disputes.

9. To obtain the name of the winner, please send your request and a self-addressed stamped envelope (excluding residents of Vermont and Washington) to THE NEW ADVENTURES OF MARY-KATE & ASHLEY Around The World Prize Pack Sweepstakes, c/o HarperEntertainment, Attn: Children's Marketing Department, 10 East 53rd Street, New York, NY 10022 by September 1, 2002. Sweepstakes Sponsor: HarperCollins Publishers, Inc.

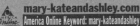

The Ultimate Fa

mary-kate

Don't miss

Reading Checklist

...ndashley

...ngle one!

TWO of a kind

It's a Twin Thing
How to Flunk
Your First Date
The Sleepover Secret
One Twin Too Many
To Snoop or Not to Snoop?
My Sister the Supermodel
Two's a Crowd
Let's Party!
Calling All Boys
Winner Take All
P. S. Wish You Were Here
The Cool Club
War of the Wardrobes
Bye-Bye Boyfriend
It's Snow Problem
Likes Me, Likes Me Not
Shore Thing
Two for the Road

❑ Surprise, Surprise
❑ Sealed With a Kiss
❑ Now You See Him, Now you Don't
❑ April Fools' Rules!

so little time

❑ How to Train a Boy
❑ Instant Boyfriend
❑ Too Good To Be True

❑ Never Been Kissed
❑ Wishes and Dreams
❑ Going My Way

Super Specials:
❑ My Mary-Kate & Ashley Diary
❑ Our Story
❑ Passport to Paris Scrapbook
❑ Be My Valentine

**Available wherever books are sold,
or call 1-800-331-3761 to order.**

Mary-Kate and Ashley'

Bestselling Book Series!

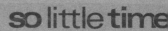

Chloe and Riley. . . So much to do. . . so little time

mary-kateandashley.com
America Online Keyword: mary-kateandashley

DUALSTAR
PUBLICATIONS

HarperEntertainment
An Imprint of HarperCollinsPublishers
www.harpercollins.com

Do you have all the Mary-Kate and Ashley books?

See the checklist to find out!